Gene's Tunes

Gene likes to sing tunes for his pals. Gene's pals are Jules, Zeke, and June.

Gene's pals stop talking when he sings. They do not want to be rude. Gene's pals love his tunes.

Gene and his pals all live in a huge spruce. They use the trunk for their homes.

Gene sings his tunes at home when he is not with his pals. Gene's mom loves when Gene sings tunes.

Zeke says that Gene should compete with others who sing tunes. Zeke thinks Gene would win!

"Yes! You're the best at singing tunes!" adds June.

"I do not think I would win," muses Gene.

Jules says, "Dude, you should compete!"

"I will think about it," says Gene.

Gene is back at home in the spruce. He tells Mom that his pals want him to compete.

"Yes, you should!" says Mom.

The next day, Gene hangs with his pals. Gene tells his pals that he will compete.

"Yes!" yells Zeke.

Gene uses all his time singing tunes. Gene's pals help too.

"You can do this!" says Jules.

Now it is time for Gene to compete.

Gene sings a long and soft tune.

"They sing nice tunes too," muses Gene.

In the end, Gene's tune wins!

Gene's pals yell, "You did it, friend!"

Phonics Fun

- Use flash cards or the list from the book.
- How fast can you read the words?
- Time yourself reading the words.
- Try to beat your time.

 High Frequency Words

live   use

 Comprehension

What would you change if you wrote the book?

 Decodable Words

compete	rude
dude	spruce
huge	tune
Jules	use
June	Zeke
muse	